For Dudley D. Watkins

First published in Great Britain
by Andersen Press Ltd in 1996
First published in Picture Lions in 1998

3 5 7 9 10 8 6 4 2

ISBN: 0 00 664522 4

Picture Lions is an imprint of the Children's
Division, part of HarperCollins Publishers Ltd,
77-85 Fulham Palace Road, Hammersmith, London W6 8JB.
Text and illustrations copyright © Colin McNaughton 1996
The author/illustrator asserts the moral right to be identified
as the author/illustrator of the work.
The HarperCollins website address is: www.fireandwater.com
Printed and bound in Singapore by Imago.

Sneaky
short cut

Colin McNaughton

Oops!

PictureLions

An Imprint of HarperCollins*Publishers*

It was the same old story.
Mister Wolf was hungry.
Mister Wolf was very hungry
and Mister Wolf had his
eye on Preston Pig.

Mister Wolf was hungry
for three very good reasons:

1. Mister Plimp the shopkeeper
had banned him from his shop
for eating the customers.

2. Mister Plump the park keeper
had banned him from the park
for picnicking on the visitors.

3. Miss Thump the school
teacher had banned him
from the school grounds
for snacking on the students.

"Don't look at me like that,
I'm the Big Bad Wolf!
It's my job to be nasty.
These stories would be
pretty boring if I was
good, wouldn't they?"

Suddenly!

There was a huge crash.
"Oops!" said Preston.

"You clumsy great pudding!" said Preston's mum. "Get out from under my feet and take that basket of food to your granny's. She's not well."

"Yes, Mum," said Preston.

"And tell Granny I'll be over later to chop her some wood," said Preston's dad.

"Yes, Dad," said Preston.

"And put your coat on," said Preston's mum.

"Yes, Mum," said Preston.

"And don't slam the door," said Preston's dad. "The chimney pot is loose..."

"Slam!" went the door.
"Oops!" went Preston.

"Hmm...red hood, basket of food, granny's house? That reminds me of a story, but which one?" said Mister Wolf - just before the chimney pot landed on his head.

Oops!

Mister Wolf picked himself up
and followed Preston.
"I'll take a short cut through
the woods and get ahead
of him," said Mister Wolf.

Sneaky
short cut

But Mister Wolf did not like
the woods. Woods were full of
nasty, itchy, scratchy, bitey things.

"I wish I could think which story that red hood reminds me of," said Mister Wolf crossly as he pulled thorns out of his bottom.

"I know it isn't *The Three Little Pigs*," said Mister Wolf. "But I do like that story. Especially the bit where the wolf eats the three little pigs and escapes. Well, that's how *my* mum used to tell it!"

Mister Wolf tried some cunning
wolf tricks to catch Preston
but he didn't have much luck.

Cunning Wolf Trick No. 1
The old 'Banana Skin' ploy.

Cunning Wolf Trick No. 2
The old 'Dig-a-Deep-Pit' dodge.

Cunning Wolf Trick No. 3
The old 'If-All-Else-Fails-Bash-'em-on-the-Head-with-a-Big-Stick' plan.

Preston reached Granny's house safely. Mister Wolf was fed up. He was hot and sticky, scratched, stung and bitten. "And I still can't remember that rotten story!" said Mister Wolf.

Suddenly!

There was a huge crash.
"Oops!" said Preston.

Mister Wolf sneaked up
to the window and this
is what he heard…

"What big eyes you've got,
Granny!" said Preston.
"All the better to see you
smash my teapot!" said Granny.

"What big ears you've got,
Granny!" said Preston.
"All the better to hear you
smash my cups!" said Granny.

"What big teeth you've got,
Granny!" said Preston.
"All the better to gnash
when you smash my sugar
bowl!" said Granny.

"Hey," cried Mister Wolf, "those are *my* lines! I remember that story now. It's *Little Red Riding Hood*." Mister Wolf leaped through the window, tied Granny up and stuffed Preston in a sack.

"Now, let me think," said Mister Wolf. "How does that story end?" He was just opening the door when he remembered…

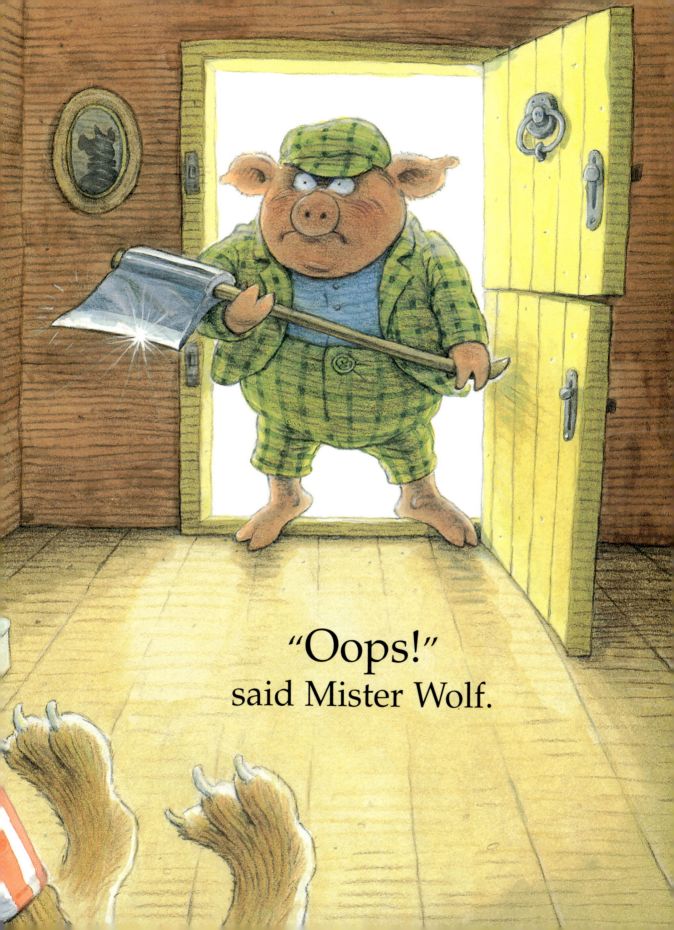

"Oops!"
said Mister Wolf.

COLIN MCNAUGHTON was born in Northumberland and had his first book published while he was still at college. He is now one of Britain's most highly acclaimed authors and illustrators of children's books and a winner of many prestigious awards, including the Kurt Maschler award in 1991. *Oops!* has added to his success, winning the 1996 Smarties Book Prize in the under-fives category.

Oops! is the third hilarious book featuring Preston the pig. The first, *Suddenly!*, was shortlisted for both the Smarties and the WH Smith/*SHE* Under-Fives awards.

SUDDENLY!
"More animated than a Tom and Jerry cartoon"
Sunday Telegraph

BOO!
"An exuberant, noisy story... Huge fun for three-to-five-year olds"
Financial Times

Look out for the next story featuring Preston and friends, to be published in Collins Picture Lions in March 1999.